D1151470

POCKET
BEARS

Methuen/Moonlight
Published originally under the title:
Na warte, sagte Schwarte, by Helme Heine
© 1977 by Gertraud Middelhauve Verlag GmbH & Co KG, Köln
First published in the United Kingdom by
Chatto & Windus Ltd 1978
First published 1984 in Pocket Bears by Methuen
Children's Books Ltd, 11 New Fetter Lane, London EC4
in association with Moonlight Publishing Ltd
131 Kensington Church Street, London W8

Printed in Italy by La Editoriale Libraria

ISBN 0 907144 61 6

The Pigs' Wedding

by Helme Heine

methuen ● moonlight

Trotter Pig built a fire and made smoke
signals that said:
Tomorrow...is...Trotter's...wedding
...day.
You...are...all...invited.

Their friends came from
far and near to be at
Trotter and Curlytail's
wedding. And Curlytail
whispered to Trotter:
"How nice our guests are!
But" — she sniffed —
"they do smell."

Trotter called to his guests: "Friends, we're glad you have come. But you have to get cleaned up for a wedding. So let me give you all a bath."
When they were all clean, Curlytail said: "Now we must dress you up!"

Trotter had forgotten all about clothes for the wedding, but he thought quickly and then said brightly: "Wait a minute," and ran off to the barn!

Trotter came back with a wheelbarrow
full of paint pots and said: "We'll paint
on our best clothes."

Each pig got just what he or she wanted, and everything fitted perfectly. The preacher's gown was comfortable over his stomach. Buttons stayed fastened, neck ties stayed tied, Trotter's cigar stayed alight.

What about his top hat?
Trotter had another good idea.
He painted an empty paint
can black . . . and put it on.

Now they were ready to have their pictures taken. The photographer had a real camera.

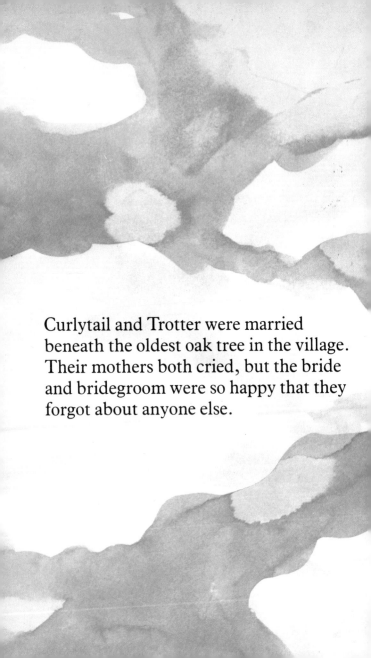

Curlytail and Trotter were married beneath the oldest oak tree in the village. Their mothers both cried, but the bride and bridegroom were so happy that they forgot about anyone else.

After the ceremony the pigs ran to the table where the feast was laid out. The wedding had made them hungry and thirsty.

Some of them ate and drank so much
that their painted clothes started to split.
But who cared about clothes when the
food tasted so good!

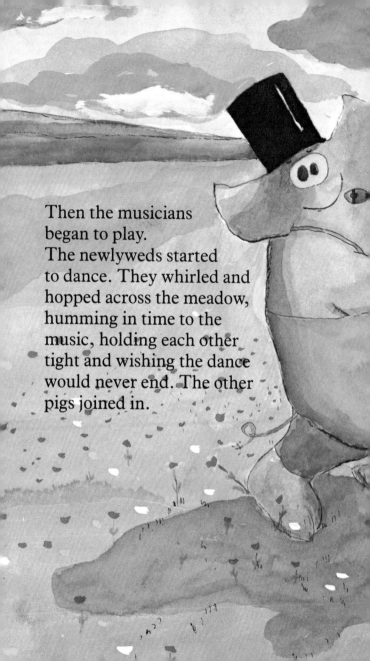

Then the musicians
began to play.
The newlyweds started
to dance. They whirled and
hopped across the meadow,
humming in time to the
music, holding each other
tight and wishing the dance
would never end. The other
pigs joined in.

They were dancing so hard that they didn't notice the black clouds gathering in the sky. Suddenly the clouds burst... The pigs ran for shelter — but too late!

The rain washed off their dresses
and suits, their pearl necklaces
and silk ties, the spectacles,
the wrist-watches, and
even Trotter's cigar.

When the rain finally stopped, Trotter said: "Stop crying, everyone. We're wet enough already. Follow me!"
He had had another brilliant idea. Running behind him, one after another, each pig took a flying leap into the mud-pond — and each, with a great SPLAT, landed right in the delicious mud.

After all their guests had left, muddy and happy, Trotter picked up Curlytail in his arms and carried her into the barn, as a bridegroom should do.

In the barn he said: "My darling
Curlytail, I have a wonderful idea!"
He pushed the straw aside and carefully
painted on the barn wall a beautiful
four-poster bed...

. . . the most beautiful bed any pig had ever seen. And, cuddled together, they fell asleep, dreaming happy pig dreams.

The end

FOR YOUNG CHILDREN

More Pocket Bears for you to enjoy!

Bill and Stanley by Helen Oxenbury
A busy afternoon for Bill and his best friend,
Stanley the dog.

Benedict Finds a Home by Chris L. Demarest
Benedict's hilarious but unsuccessful attempts to
find a nest away from his noisy brothers and sisters.

This Little-Pig-a-Wig by Lenore and Erik Blegvad
Familiar and less-known pig poems and nursery rhymes.

Billy Goat and His Well-Fed Friends by Nonny Hogrogian
"Billy Goat is getting fat. He will soon be ready
for us to eat."
"Not if I can help it!" said Billy Goat.
An I Can Read Book.

In Summer When I Go to Bed by Juan Winijgaard
Delightful short poems for summer evenings or any dreamy moments.

There's a Nightmare in my Cupboard by Mercer Mayer
A reassuring monster tale, to tame any nightmare and laugh a lot.

Honey Bear by Erika Dietzsch-Capelle
Kind, cuddly Honey Bear one day has to learn to be tough too.

Animal Babies by H. Baumann and E. Dietzsch-Capelle
How do they play? How do they sleep? The delightful habits
and antics of many baby animals.

Peter and the Wolf by Sergei Prokofiev and Erna Voigt
The well-known musical tale, beautifully illustrated.

Walk Rabbit Walk by Colin McNaughton
and Elizabeth Attenborough
Maybe it's wiser to walk like Rabbit than to
fly, drive or rollerskate like his friends.

Get Along, Old Trapper by Stephen Gammell
A true tale of the Wild West with adventurous old Jack the Trapper.

Santa's Crash-Bang Christmas by Steven Kroll
and Tomie de Paola
A very clumsy Father Christmas brings havoc to a peaceful house...

FOR CHILDREN BEGINNING TO READ CONFIDENTLY

Mr Potter's Pigeon by Reg Cartwright
*The moving story of an old man and his pet
racing pigeon; award-winning pictures.*

King Nonn the Wiser by Colin McNaughton
The hilarious adventures of a brave but short-sighted knight.

The Pigs' Wedding by Helme Heine
A day full of surprises, fun and happiness for Trotter and Curlytail.

The Friends' Racing Cart by Helme Heine
*Johnny Mouse's friends are quick to the rescue when his fast cart
goes out of control.*

Hare and Badger Go to Town by Naomi Lewis and Tony Ross
The modern fable of how Hare and Badger fare with city life.

Jack and the Beanstalk by Tony Ross
*One of Tony Ross' best-known revivals of
traditional fairy tales.*

The Greedy Little Cobbler by Tony Ross
Why the little cobbler is the worst shod of all.

The Little Moon Theatre by Irene Haas
The troop of travelling players makes wishes come true…

The Hairy Monster by Henriette Bichonnier and Pef
*Little Princess Lucy is cheeky but far cleverer than the horrible
Hairy Monster who wants to gobble her up.*

Panda's Puzzle by Michael Foreman
*Panda travels from the Himalayas to the United States
to find the answer to a very important question.*

Lola at the Riverbank and
Lola and the Dandelion Mystery by Yvan Pommaux
*In these two enchanting books, Lola the little vole asks
her father questions about nature that intrigue all children.*

See You in the Morning! and
The Higher and Higher House by Janosch
*Each title contains several short tales about Snoddle and his friends,
full of comical details, riddles and games.*